Salam Alaikum

(suh-LAM ah-LEY-ee-koom).

Peace be upon you.

(informal)

Assalamu Alaikum

(ahh-suh-LAM-ooh ah-LEY-ee-koom).

Peace be upon you.

(formal)

FOR EVERY KID WORLDWIDE DREAMING OF PEACE—H. J.

TO MY FAMILY, MY FRIENDS, EVERYONE—I AM DEEPLY INSPIRED BY ALL OF YOU—W. J.

SALAAM
R E A D S

An imprint of Simon & Schuster Children's Publishing Division

1230 Avenue of the Americas, New York, New York 10020

Text copyright © 2015 by Awakening Worldwide Ltd.

Illustrations copyright © 2017 by Ward Jenkins

All rights reserved, including the right of reproduction in whole or in part in any form.

SALAAM READS and its logo are trademarks of Simon & Schuster, Inc.

For information about special discounts for bulk purchases, please contact Simon & Schuster Special Sales

at 1-866-506-1949 or business@simonandschuster.com.

The Simon & Schuster Speakers Bureau can bring authors to your live event. For more information

or to book an event, contact the Simon & Schuster Speakers Bureau at 1-866-248-3049

or visit our website at www.simonspeakers.com.

Book design by Lucy Ruth Cummins

The text for this book was set in Galano Classic.

The illustrations for this book were rendered digitally.

Manufactured in China

0617 SCP

First Edition

2 4 6 8 10 9 7 5 3 1

CIP data for this book is available from the Library of Congress.

ISBN 978-1-4814-8938-6

ISBN 978-1-4814-8939-3 (eBook)

Salam Alaikum

Words by HARRIS J   Pictures by WARD JENKINS

SALAAM
R E A D S

NEW YORK | LONDON | TORONTO
SYDNEY | NEW DELHI

You can try to turn off the sun,

I'm still going to shine away

and tell everyone

we're having some fun today.

We can go wherever you want to
and do whatever you like.

Let's just have a
real good time.

Assalamu Alaikum.

I just want to spread love and peace
and all of my happiness

to everyone that I meet
'cause I'm feeling spectacular.

I love it when we love one another.

Give thanks every day

for this life, living with
a smile on my face.

Assalamu Alaikum.

Spread peace on the Earth.

Cherish the love that is around us.

Spread peace on the Earth.

Treasure the love, let it surround us.

Always be kind, always remind one another:

peace on the Earth every day.

Assalamu

Alaikum.

Wa Alaikuma Salam
(wah ah-LEY-ee-koom-ah suh-LAM).
And upon
you peace.